Praise for *How to Get Your Fucking Money Back*

"A challenging volume that delivers neither on its title nor its purpose; presuming its title indicates what it's supposed to be about and its purpose is entertainment."

- Lee Harvey Oswald, Jr. (no relation)

"I curse both the author and the reader for their complicity in this. A real slap in the tits."

- I Can't Believe It's Not The National Review of Books

"This book belongs in the recycling bin with the rest of America's liberal garbage."

- Mister Bones, drive-time radio host, 105.9 Lite FM

"When reading this, I felt the same way a kid feels when they see an adult picking their nose. It's like everything we've been taught means nothing."

- Becky Gelke, influencee

Also by Scott Ritcher

Slamdek A to Z: The Illustrated History of Louisville's Slamdek Record Company (1996)

Letters to Saint Clinton (2004)

K Composite Magazine (1991–2016)

Gone With the Wind, Part 2 (1952)

Model Railroading Disasters (1972)

The King James Bible with Jokes (1988)

Wi-Fi Sickness and Other As-Yet-Undiagnosed Conditions of the Modern Era (2018)

Poetry for Stupid Fuckers (2019)

HOW TO GET YOUR FUCKING MONEY BACK

K Composite

K Composite Media
Post Office Box 43551
Louisville, Kentucky 40253 USA

kcomposite.com

ISBN 978-0-9882663-6-0

FIRST EDITION

This page is set in Baskerville to make it more believable.[1] The rest of the main text is set in Savoy to make it more beautiful. Chapter titles are in Behemoth CG. Drop caps are in Beastly. The sub-chapter titles are in Sentinel Black. That amazing font on the cover is ITC Serif Gothic Heavy, designed in New York in 1972 by Herb Lublin and Tony DeSpigna.

---

[1] Errol Morris, "Hear, All Ye People; Hearken, O Earth," *The New York Times*, August 8, 2012

For reading

Contents

(and spoilers)

PRESIDENTIAL FUN FACTS & TRIVIA

For my beautiful wife,
Kirsten Dunst

Your love of presidential history
has been a constant inspiration
on this journey

Preface

The first line of a book is the most important one. This fact was never more true than in the case of my seminal work, *Presidential Fun Facts & Trivia*.

But enough about me. Let's talk about the presidents.

There have been several presidents in America and some of their lives have had events you don't know about. I don't care who you are, but you don't know everything. Thus, your ignorance and that exhibited by others of your ilk are part and parcel to why I have exhaustively researched and compiled this keepsake collection.

It is my hope that this book will help shed light upon the generations of great Americans who came before us. Their tireless work in pursuit of liberty for white men made it possible for us to fight for equality.

The Founding Fathers never could have imagined they were laying such fertile groundwork for their descendants who would still be trying to correct their errors more than two centuries later. They certainly didn't fathom the possibility of a gun that fires a hundred bullets in five seconds, nor what it would be like if they gave everyone the right to own such a magnificent machine, including lonely losers and big, dumb jackasses.

In short, they really blew it on many accounts, and the decades of struggle that continue today were inspired by their lack of foresight. We truly couldn't have done it without them.

If I may postulate in their defense, many of the Founding Fathers were wholly unprepared[2] for what they were doing and the repercussions their decisions and compromises would have. The thought of us knowing their

---

[2] Though unfair, some choose to judge our ancestors by today's standards. For instance, Lincoln wasn't even vegan and Franklin didn't sort his recyclables.

names would have blown their minds. These guys were still bouncing off the walls, reeling and *totes psyched*[3] in the realization that they had actually accomplished the highly unlikely goal of attaining their independence. They hardly had time to celebrate before they were hit in the guts with another monumental task.

Thomas Jefferson captured the gravity of the moment in a letter to Gen. George Washington, "Guess we gotta start a country now, huh? How does one even do that?" The scope of the undertaking at hand wasn't lost on Washington, who, days later, replied in a winter missive, "You worry too much, Tom. We wing it. I give us six years (*tops!*) before we're all in a filthy British prison.[4] Just hope our cells are near each other. If not, I'd really miss you."

---

[3] Very excited

[4] They were writing these letters in old-timey days, so some of their S's looked like F's. It was actually a soft S, known as the *long S* or *medial S*. (You know, so it looks like *fubject* instead of *subject*.) For the sake of modern readability, we have fixed that nonfenfe. Ferioufly.

To which Jefferson replied not a fortnight[5] later, "Probably right. What are the chances that we're gonna get away with *any* of this? Aside from missing you, I think what I'd miss most is all the great people I own."

Yet, *Presidential Fun Facts & Trivia* is a volume that is not limited just to those few Founding Fathers who later served as President. As you'll discover, this collection spans the entire succession of every single president who served from March of 1885 all the way through to the beginning of 1889.

I suspect this reference companion shall appeal equally to the wide-eyed schoolchildren[6] who lament its assignment as

---

[5] 14 days. Roughly equivalent to two weeks on today's calendars.
[6] Fuckin' kids. Ugh.

required reading, as it will to the casual buffs of history who leaf through its pages on lazy afternoons; perhaps whilst relaxing, perhaps whilst pooping, perhaps while simply teaching a masterclass on the English language.

Indeed, despite this publication's breadth of particulars, its compact size and portability are no accident. For this volume was designed to be carried along to anywhere one might wish to learn a bit more about the presidents. I don't know about you, dear reader, but in my world, why, that is just about anywhere. Yes, just about anywhere indeed.

The future scholars[7] who study this treatise will likely find inspiration in these pages for furthering their own research. In such cases, I consider the sweat, toil and sleepless minutes that my dedicated team[8] of research assistants and I put into this

---

[7] Probably living in space or at least wearing cool clothes with angular lines and reflective accents

[8] Unpaid interns who didn't even get college credit because I sent the forms in too late and I described their work using somewhat regrettable language

effort to be a success, long before the first drop of ink was set to this paper.

Regardless of your purpose in exploring all manner of the fun facts and trivia to be found within these pages, it is with some small degree of humility that I wish you much success on your journey into presidential history.

Col. Scott Ritcher III
Chairman and chief executive
General Motors Corporation
Tampon, California, 1952

Sent from my iPhone

Presidential Fun Facts & Trivia

Grover Cleveland was the only president to be wed while in office. His marriage ceremony with Frances Folsom was held at the White House in June of 1886.

This page intentionally left blank[9]

---

[9] Well, we left it blank except for the part where we explained that it was left blank on purpose. And you're right, it also has a page number and this footnote, of course. And that little line above the footnote. But we made every effort to print all this as small as we could in order to honor this page and our original intention of leaving it blank. We still feel that blank was the best way to go; or at least what we have here, which is as blank as possible given the circumstances.

Reference

1. Bird
2. Bird
3. Bird
4. Bird
5. Bird
6. Bird
7. Bird
8. Bird
9. Bird
10. Bird
11. Bird
12. Bird
13. Bird
14. Bird
15. Bird
16. Bird
17. Bird
18. Bird
19. Bird
20. Bird
21. Bird
22. Bird

Adjective Thermometer Conversion Table

Convert temperatures from Fahrenheit or Celsius to adjectives without the Adjective Thermometer application

°F	°C	Adjective	°F	°C	Adjective
-20	-28.9	lost	10	-12.2	worthless
-19	-28.3	just fucked	11	-11.7	imbecilic
-18	-27.8	out of control	12	-11.1	idiotic
-17	-27.2	mismanaged	13	-10.6	irrational
-16	-26.7	remorseless	14	-10.0	moronic
-15	-26.1	dead	15	-9.4	brazen
-14	-25.6	lost	16	-8.9	laughable
-13	-25.0	DOA	17	-8.3	insulting
-12	-24.4	irredeemable	18	-7.8	rude
-11	-23.9	irreversible	19	-7.2	absurd
-10	-23.3	freakish	20	-6.7	objectionable
-9	-22.8	terminal	21	-6.1	inadmissible
-8	-22.2	unacceptable	22	-5.6	farcical
-7	-21.7	fucked up	23	-5.0	out of line
-6	-21.1	degrading	24	-4.4	silly
-5	-20.6	hopeless	25	-3.9	unfriendly
-4	-20.0	meaningless	26	-3.3	unsympathetic
-3	-19.4	illogical	27	-2.8	frightful
-2	-18.9	absurd	28	-2.2	ungrateful
-1	-18.3	injurious	29	-1.7	demeaning
1	-17.2	irrational	30	-1.1	indiscreet
2	-16.7	irrational	31	-0.6	sarcastic
3	-16.1	forsaking	32	0.0	relinquishing
4	-15.6	humiliating	33	0.6	cowardly
5	-15.0	ridiculing	34	1.1	disappointing
6	-14.4	witless	35	1.7	derogatory
7	-13.9	insolent	36	2.2	irreverent
8	-13.3	pointless	37	2.8	impolite
9	-12.8	hostile	38	3.3	ungracious

°F	°C	Adjective	°F	°C	Adjective
39	3.9	lacking	80	26.7	energizing
40	4.4	discourteous	81	27.2	provocative
41	5.0	uninviting	82	27.8	lush
42	5.6	unrewarding	83	28.3	amusing
43	6.1	deficient	84	28.9	unrestrained
44	6.7	subpar	85	29.4	significant
45	7.2	trivial	86	30.0	anxious
46	7.8	inferior	87	30.6	overzealous
47	8.3	unproductive	88	31.1	irritable
48	8.9	hesitant	89	31.7	intimate
49	9.4	indecisive	90	32.2	too eager
50	10.0	tolerable	91	32.8	powerful
51	10.6	passable	92	33.3	bold
52	11.1	admissible	93	33.9	intense
53	11.7	teasing	94	34.4	loud
54	12.2	sympathetic	95	35.0	futile
55	12.8	conciliatory	96	35.6	fierce
56	13.3	reassuring	97	36.1	troublesome
57	13.9	civil	98	36.7	extreme
58	14.4	hopeful	99	37.2	nonsensical
59	15.0	satisfactory	100	37.8	laughable
60	15.6	courteous	101	38.3	profane
61	16.1	considerate	102	38.9	obnoxious
62	16.7	receptive	103	39.4	contemptuous
63	17.2	agreeable	104	40.0	unamusing
64	17.8	diplomatic	105	40.6	unacceptable
65	18.3	cordial	106	41.1	crazy
66	18.9	reasonable	107	41.7	ludicrous
67	19.4	gracious	108	42.2	outrageous
68	20.0	respectful	109	42.8	preposterous
69	20.6	amiable	110	43.3	insane
70	21.1	polite	111	43.9	hellish
71	21.7	welcoming	112	44.4	repulsive
72	22.2	friendly	113	45.0	dictatorial
73	22.8	endearing	114	45.6	abusive
74	23.3	thrilling	115	46.1	murderous
75	23.9	appreciative	116	46.7	dangerous
76	24.4	gratifying	117	47.2	deadly
77	25.0	generous	118	47.8	lethal
78	25.6	affectionate	119	48.3	impossible
79	26.1	rapturous	120	48.9	toxic

This page unintentionally left blank.

This was not at all intentional. It was a big fucking mistake.

There was supposed to be a cool picture of two astronauts fighting here, but great, we've got another blank page instead.

Believe me, several people got fired over this.

Listen, we know they all had families and
one of them had a sick kid at home and it was
right before Christmas, but a blank page is a blank page,
and if you can't get that through your thick fucking skull, then
maybe this isn't really the place for you. Maybe we're just not a
good fit. Is Don on the phone? I mean, we'll write you a letter of
recommendation and all that kind of stuff, but there's a difference
between a page that *should* have ink on it and one that *shouldn't*.
These are unspoken things. Everybody knows this. Joe Gutenberg
knew this. At this point, we *seriously* would have expected *you*
and the rest of your lot to know what we intended. I mean, did
you *all* really think page 32 should be blank? Honestly? Ugh.
Anyone else here who thought page 32 should be left blank?
Speak up. What? *Both of you?* Oh, come on. You cannot
be serious. Get outta here, all of you. Miss Davidson,
can you escort these turkeys to the front gate?
Yeah, yeah. Merry Christmas to you, too.

Everybody Knows This

There are very few things that everyone agrees on. These are unspoken things.

Most people eat dinner, and when they do, it happens later in the day than noon.

Everybody knows this.

Sometimes I eat breakfast. Rarely, but sometimes. It would be a surprise to see a standard breakfast table setting near me, unless I were at a hotel. When I'm at home, the coffee is there, yes. But the juice glass, the multiple plates and three utensils? I don't think so.

Despite living in Europe, I think even my fellow Europeans would agree that the European table settings are overkill. You just don't need nine utensils and four glasses to eat dinner. Everybody knows this, but only some of us are brave enough to admit it.

Table Settings

Breakfast

Lunch

Dinner

European

Here's the Tower (exhibit)

About the Author

by ███████████, *picnic planner[10] and
founder of Old Glory Whole Wheat Bread[11]*

Dr. Prescott "Scott" Hussein "Scott" Ritcher, Jr., was a prolific writer and a lot like Ernest Hemingway in many respects. Well, like Hemingway without the talent, wives, bravery, adventure and success. Basically, just the alcoholism and the man boobs. So just three respects.

He was born in the rustic shanty town of Narragansett, Rhode Island, during the brutal winter of 1984. (Ritcher, that is. Hemingway was born much earlier in Oak Park, Illinois.[12])

---

[10] Amateur

[11] *Here's the Tower*, episode 12, "Hank Williams, Jr., and the Great Zoo Robbery, Part 3," August 8, 2018 https://kcomposite.com/hank-williams-jr-and-the-great-zoo-robbery-part-3

[12] For more information about Ernest Hemingway, visit your local library.

The fourth and only child of a pauper and paupress, Ritcher's youth was filled with painting dead trees and the unabating documentation of such silly acts in service to the possibility that someone in the distant future should require those resources for a museum collection.[13]

To be clear, he wasn't painting *pictures* of dead trees, he was applying paint directly to the bark of dead trees in order to change their color. There was a particular shade of dusty violet that amused him.

After years of fairly hilarious misbehavior, young Scott's teachers and parents finally tired of his antics and made the very easy decision to send him away.

Sources tell me their deliberations at an emergency parent-teacher meeting went something to the effect of:

---

[13] As of the date of this publication, no such museum exists.

"Are you all thinking what I'm thinking?"

"God, I hope so."

"Alright, then. It's settled."

[Awkward pause and a moment of everyone looking around the room]

"Should we get some coffee, or...?"

Despite the fact that his arrival at the True Value Boarding School - located in a town that I'll fill in here later after I think of something funny - was somewhat unceremonious, it was there that he learned his famously fine manners and studied proper European table settings.[14] (Knives then spoons on the right, forks on the left. Like I need to tell *you* this. Readers of a heady compendium such as this are no doubt well versed in the etiquette of international place settings.)

It was during young Ritcher's absence at boarding school that his parents became swingers.

---

[14] For more information about European place settings, please see the earlier chapter titled Table Settings. Honestly, even if you didn't previously know how to set a table, you should have discovered that nugget before you got to this page. I guess I should have told you earlier that this book is intended to be read in its traditional sequence, at least the first time.

And again, like I need to tell *you* this. There are more people who know about the Ritcher parents being swingers than there are people who know how to properly set a table in Europe.

To his swinging parents' dismay, young Scott didn't last long at True Value. Following his untimely (but well-deserved) expulsion from boarding school, the lad hopped a plane and enlisted in the Belgian National Guard.[15] It was funny at the time, yet it became less so immediately. I can't say I recommend it. You have to make your own bed - *every single day* - and they yell at you and make you do stuff.

---

[15] It wasn't quite the French Foreign Legion, but he didn't know what that was, so it was all the same to him. French fries probably originated in Belgium (or Spain), so he probably would have thought the Foreign Legion was also a bunch of phonies trying to be someone else. You know, like if an American moves to Sweden and learns their language, or some poser shit like that.

It wasn't long[16] before his mind wandered again and he began to find the entire objective of protecting the Belgian homeland to be imprudent. The chances were slim that anyone would actually want to invade the New Jersey of Europe, so the boy saw no point in continuing to sacrifice his precious time to be one of its guardians.

The eight-month ordeal ended with a dishonorable discharge after he had overstayed his leaves one too many times, chasing after a wild but stylish Flemish girl by the name of Annabel van de Velde. (She was much more casual and unassuming than her name would lead you to believe. It's a pretty common surname in the Flanders region of Belgium.)

With black-rimmed cat-eye glasses, a small, turned-up nose, a penchant for wearing summery tank tops and reddish-brown braids whose ends brushed her bare shoulders when she turned her

---

[16] It was six months. I'd say that isn't long, but if you're bored or heartbroken it can be an eternity. Am I right, people? The Smiths only made so many records and everything loses its impact if you overuse it.

head, Ritcher thought she was well worth being declared AWOL.

He couldn't keep his hands off those delicate clavicles[17] and she couldn't get enough of having his freckled arm around her, resting his hand on her soft, tanned shoulder as they bar hopped and stumbled their way through Ghent.

Day after day, sunny afternoons turned to cool evenings until it didn't matter much if he would be kicked out of the service.

Yet as soon as he was free of the Guard, Annabel lost interest in him all but forthwith. The danger and excitement was gone when she knew she could have him. There was no trouble to get into anymore, and for her, the sparks and butterflies went as well.

Heartbroken and Belgian francless, he caught the slow boat out of Ghent, making his way to an even slower slow boat in

---

[17] *Mmmmph! Damn, girl!*

Antwerp that carried him back to the States.[18] The stormy journey to Providence aboard the SS *Columbia*[19] took nearly a month and a half as the old steam ship was tossed – sometimes violently – across the ocean.

To pass time on the trip, Ritcher buried himself in books about the American presidents from the ship's library, drank hot tea from the galley, wrote frantically about how matching socks are a hoax[20] and occasionally played cards, shuffleboard and dice with retirees and the staff – anything to wipe his mind clean of any memories of Annabel, that nose and those sweet, sweet collarbones.

---

[18] Pro tip: Almost nobody who is *from* the United States calls it "the States." They call it "America" or "the U.S."

[19] Originally christened the SS *Belgenland* when she was launched in 1914 by the International Mercantile Marine Company's Belgium-based Red Star Line, she was renamed to the *Belgic* in 1917 by the International Navigation Company. Her name was changed back in 1923 and she sailed under her original name until she was purchased by the Atlantic Transport Company of West Virginia in 1935. At that point she was finally named the SS *Columbia*. Although nautical records show that she was scrapped in Alaska in 1936, Ritcher swears this was the ocean liner he took to Rhode Island. But he was pretty out of his mind thanks to being all hung up on ol' What's-her-name.

[20] Socks are manufactured individually, then paired together later.

Flash's! Car Wash, Chicago (the one in Illinois)

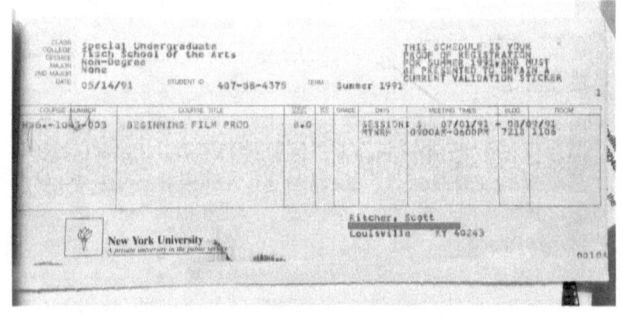

Beginning Film Production course schedule, New York
University, summer 1991

Always Be Suspicious of a Guy Wearing Jewelry and a Track Suit

In 1978, Ritcher found himself listless and somewhat dispirited, while studying to be a gentleman forester at the Southwestern Bible Institute[21] in Waxahachie, Texas. In his malaise, he made a list of pros and cons for completing his studies. As the list of cons grew quickly, a scant few items materialized in the pro column.

As if scheduled by some sort of cosmic timer, a visitor rasped upon the door. When Ritcher creaked his dorm room door[22] open, two friends stood there holding their own pro-and-con lists. Those friends were none other than Burger

---

[21] This is the same school where 14-year-old Jerry Lee Lewis was expelled after three months for "performing a rowdy version of 'My God Is Real' at a church assembly."

[22] "Dorm room door" is a 12-character phrase containing just three letters. It's 14 characters if you include the spaces.

Reynolds, a chef, and Reynolds' roommate and associate, Burger Jeff. They had come to ask Ritcher to join them as they launched Burger Chef, an innovative new restaurant chain where the burgers would be wrapped in plastic instead of paper.

None of these three fools had any business going into the restaurant business.[23]

Ritcher, for one, was the mortal enemy of food. At any Asian restaurant when asked how spicy he wanted his dish, he would always reply, simply, "Ruin it." He was never happy with the food unless it was so spicy that his nose was running and he was crying into a profuse case of the old-man sweats. Even before he turned 25, the old-man sweats were in full effect.

---

[23] I just wanna say, y'all... I really hate that this sentence has the word "business" in it twice, but I seriously couldn't think of a different way to say it. Maybe we can fix this in the second edition. No refunds.

"How are you enjoying your meal? Can I get you some more water?" a server would ask him, purely out of safety concerns.

"Take this back to the kitchen," he would command as if he were Nixon. "Make it spicier. I can still feel my existence."

Burger Jeff was the kind of small-town asshole who gets a fancy car and hangs out with it in the parking lot of his high school rival's less successful restaurant.[24] He wore a black track suit with white stripes down the sides[25] on most days, zipped up with a gold chain on the outside of the collar. He had big rings from behind which the puffy meat of his sausage fingers generously overflowed.

Most alarmingly, he wore sunglasses when it was wholly unnecessary. Sunglasses adorned his stupid face[26] when it was too cloudy, too late into the evening and too long after he had been inside

---

[24] A real Billy Mitchell type

[25] It was supposed to look like Adidas, but it had four stripes and it was some off-brand thing from Zayre or something.

[26] The upside to him wearing sunglasses was that they covered some of his stupid face.

The Original Brand Original Brand New York 1936 Est. '36
Since 1936

Lots of words

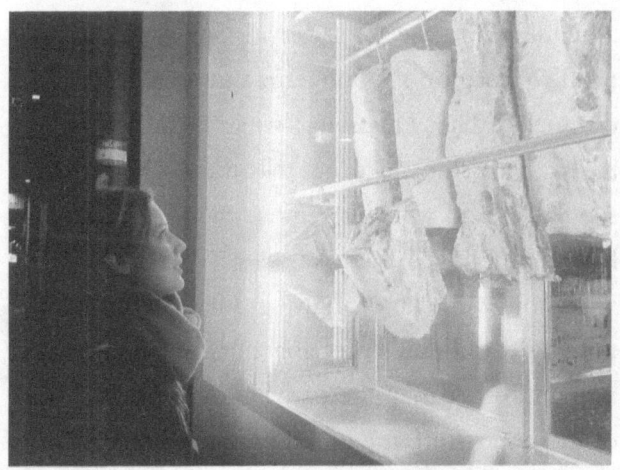

Lots of meat

Lots of cheese

a building. He was even wearing sunglasses in his profile photo on the company's internal Slack channel.[27] What I'm saying is that most people have a natural instinct that tells them when to wear sunglasses and when to remove them. Jeff didn't have that. He still doesn't.

I know we're kind of giving Burger Jeff a hard time here and that's probably not fair on any account, other than the parking lot business. Most of the other stuff amounted to his personal style choices, and while *we* might not agree with what he thought was cool, he had/has[28] every right to dress however he wants to and in a way that expresses his personality. Maybe he has sensitive eyes and needs to wear sunglasses more than so-called "normal" people. Maybe he has always been proud of his workplace and wants to let that

---

[27] He also wore the ID lanyard from his office when he went out to lunch. He was one of *those* people. But it's a big world and there are a lot of Patagonia vests out there. We have bigger problems.

[28] As of press time, the publisher has been unable to verify if Burger Jeff is still alive or still dressing like an asshole.

lanyard advertise his involvement (see footnote 27 about his lanyard).

Regardless, the restaurant business proved to be even more challenging for these jokers than it is for people who know stuff about food.

And I know what you're going to say; what about Burger Reynolds? How could *he* not know anything about food? He was a chef, after all.[29] That much is true, but the background of how he became a chef is much too sordid to get into in a book of this size that is about something else entirely (the presidents).

---

[29] He certainly knew enough to offer a pretzel bun on his burgers. "Pretzel buns are a restaurant's secret weapon," he once wrote in a *Louisville Times* op-ed. "Any restaurant that doesn't offer a pretzel bun simply doesn't care about their customers." However, a discount fast-food chain that wraps its burgers in plastic – like Burger Chef – just wasn't the appropriate venue for such an upscale item. Reynolds knew they couldn't offer a pretzel bun at their target price point, so he held his tongue and never suggested it. But he knew. Oh yes, he certainly knew.

I also have a feeling you're thinking something else; is this really how a semicolon is supposed to be used? As far as that matter is concerned, I simply don't know. If my editor lets it slip through to the print edition, I think we'll both have our answer. *[I'm not getting paid enough to deal with this shit. - Ed.]*

Ritcher went all in, investing $14.25 he had saved up[30] doing odd jobs at school and the burger chain expanded at an enthusiastic clip. It topped out at 1,050 locations just before the newly knighted[31] Sir Ritcher cashed out of the company in late 1979.

Much later, in 2020, as the world found itself in the grips of the pandemic,[32] as customers had been desperately missing the savory taste of real

---

[30] Worth the equivalent of more than $14.30 the following year.

[31] Historians and biographers are in disagreement as to whether Count Fangburger had the authority to bestow knighthood, and if so, whether such a title carried legal significance outside the grounds of his haunted hotel.

[32] The one that was brought on by coronavirus disease (COVID-19) which was caused by severe acute respiratory syndrome coronavirus 2 (SARS-CoV-2)

bats, Burger Chef introduced an all-plant-based Impossible Bat™ [33] in its restaurants. Demand was through the roof. Had Ritcher stayed with the company another 43 years, his payout would have been in the billions.

But no matter, Sir Ritcher had left the company four decades earlier to pursue his interest in acting.

---

[33] Marketed as Beyond Bat™ in Europe

Courthouse Press Member (uncredited)

Ritcher's acting success was nearly immediate. In 1994,[34] he shot to world stardom as a result of his portrayal of Atticus Finch in the hit film *Step Brothers*, for which he earned an Oscar nomination in the category of movie acting. He also painted houses, wink wink, if you catch my drift.[35]

That role was followed by another star turn in Michael Mann's *The Insider*. This based-on-real-life dramatic feature – nominated for Best Picture at the 72nd Academy Awards – starred Russell Crowe as tobacco-industry whistleblower Jeffrey Wigand and Al Pacino[36] as *60 Minutes* producer Lowell

---

[34] It's possible that the timeline of this book doesn't make any sense. We might have just skipped 15 years.

[35] Is this thing on? Can you tell I'm wearing a wire?

[36] Mr. Pacino shortened his first name for show business. His real name is Alfredo. Really.

Bergman, alongside Ritcher who stole the show as a newspaper photographer in the background of a scene where a guy was talking on the phone.
(Note: this scene might have been removed if you saw the version that was edited for Mormons and other pussies.)

The role of newspaper photographer appealed to the idealist in young Ritcher. He loved the romance of the newspaper business, yearned for the glory days of publishing - longed for the bustling newsroom: pined for the tireless writers and heated editorial meetings; had day dream about the smell of fresh ink, and paper - and a morning truckload of bundled copies of the latest edition - and the seasoned editors, who would know how to fix everything that was wrong with this sentence. *[Ugh. - Ed.]*

Principal filming for *The Insider* took place in Louisville, Kentucky, a city larger than Gothenburg but smaller than Stockholm. It's the hometown of Muhammad Ali, the Kentucky Derby, some popular baseball bats, the "Happy Birthday" song and bourbon whiskey. He had certainly heard the song before and even knew some of the words, but otherwise didn't know much about the city or the surrounding state that it apparently isn't the capital of. He had his doubts about spending so much time in Louisville, and mulling over them was what was on his mind during the 15-hour drive south from Rhode Island.

Those doubts somehow began to subside a few miles after he passed the sign "Welcome to Kentucky: As Seen on *Unsolved Mysteries.*" The storied allure of lush, green oak trees started to comfort him, and the hazy, summer bluegrass began to bewitch him. Yes, the 37th largest state by area had hooked him, and hooked him but good. Mmm hmm. Real good.

The Art of Being a Journalist When Nothing Is Happening

Working long days, side by side with Pacino and Crowe,[37] Ritcher knew he had to deliver a solid, professional performance. To prepare himself for the role of Courthouse Press Member (uncredited),[38] Ritcher immersed himself in newspaper culture. He could be found hobnobbing with local editors in the early mornings, sipping coffee with them at the Journalists' Club, a cozy café around the corner from the offices and presses of *The Louisville Times*. Then, later in the afternoons, when the late deadlines had been filed, he bounced around town with beat reporters.

---

[37] None of the actors mentioned here were present during the eight hours Ritcher was on set.

[38] IMDB, https://www.imdb.com/name/nm4769474, retrieved April 3, 2023

One of their favorite haunts was Abendschule which, despite its tongue-in-cheek international name – it's the German word for "night school" – was the kind of characterless bar that has fluorescent-tube lighting and crappy pool tables, sells bright green shots in skinny glasses and is outfitted with too many large TV screens that alternately show college basketball games or run slideshows of the bartenders and regulars drinking those shots, as well as large graphics of their drink specials. Every graphic in those slideshows and every sign in the place looked like it was made with Font Randomizer.

But the go-to watering hole for staff writers was a rowdy but hip bar called The Sun-dried Rubber Band Company. In the gritty heart of Louisville's former rubber band district, it occupied the expansive lobby and front rooms of an old rubber band factory, keeping the name, signage and 1940s interior aesthetics of its original tenant.

Happy hours often bled into all-nighters at Sun-dried (as everyone called it) and Ritcher preferred the atmosphere and lively clientele here as compared with Abendschule. A number of eccentric columnists did, too, including print-media veterans like Armond Pastore and Helen Logsdon.

When local alternative bands played on weekends, the place would be packed with raucous crowds of people from all drinking-eligible ages and backgrounds; smartly dressed but with a certain working-class toughness. Sun-dried attracted people who cared about their appearance, but who never overdid it. They looked good and smelled good, but you could tell they were also interested in each other. There was a great sense of comfort and community in this place.

All People Are Normal People in the Right Circumstances

I'll never forget the first night I met drive-time radio personality Mister Bones at Sun-dried. While waiting at the bar to order a drink with my girlfriend,[39] we heard an unmistakable voice ordering beside me. *Afternoon*

---

[39] Well, my girlfriend at the time... Birdley... who reliably wore black skirts with black tights and Doc Martens, but always something different and awesome up top... who I was crazy about... and I thought she was *the one*... well, it didn't matter much anyway, because sometime around the leave-Britney-alone era she ran off with some stupid Roy Acuff-lookin' mother-fucker who owned a small chain of convenience stores and was much older, but I have no doubt also much more capable of satisfying her in ways I could neither afford nor imagine. But that's the breaks, man. Sure, I lived to find love again, and I wouldn't trade the experiences I've had since then, but I still think about Birdley Mae Claudins from time to time, and the fun adventures we had, like that night we first met Mister Bones at Sun-dried! I should tell you about that sometime.

Mayhem with Mister Bones on 105.9 Lite FM[40]
had been a staple of life in Louisville for as long as
I could remember, and when we heard that voice,
Birdley and I looked at each other with open
mouths and our eyes got wider than we thought
they could go.

Birdley did a tight, little, two-footed dance of
excitement and that attempt at contained
commotion caught his attention. As she laughed
embarrassedly and tried to reel in her enthusiasm,
Mister Bones himself – in *that voice* – turned and
asked us what we wanted to drink!

Birdley wiped the panic off her face in an
instant and blasted the charm up to 11. She smiled
brightly and through those teeth she winked, "A
PBR and an Old Fashioned with Knob Creek."

"And what does *he* want?" Bones joked,
nodding toward me.

We cracked up. Man, he was really fast with
that line.

---

[40] *Here's the Tower*, episode 5, "And the Hits Just Keep On
Coming," June 20, 2018
https://kcomposite.com/and-the-hits-just-keep-on-coming

"The Old Fashioned is for him," she laughed. "I'll have the Pabst."

An early packaging label from Louisville's Sun-dried Rubber Band factory. The bar adopted the company's name and kept its signage in tact, and they used the old logo on their coasters, matchbooks, napkins and social media posts.

The ironically named Abendschule was known for its cheap drinks, debauchery and utter lack of charm, all of which were exactly what its regulars and college students wanted.

He laughed, too, and relayed our order to
Phil,[41] one of the always-there bartenders who

---

[41] Phil was constantly ribbed for the *one time* he had a splitting
headache and asked if anyone had any "*ibupropen.*" But it was
all in good fun and he thought it was as funny as everyone else
did. "Well, how the *hell* do you say it, then?"

Phil has since passed away and there were some sad days at
Sun-dried after that happened. It turns out he was even older
than we suspected. His father was actually employed on the
factory floor of the rubber band plant when Phil was a kid,
then climbed his way up to a sales management position. The
sales team had worked in the selfsame room where bands now
took the stage on weekends. Phil had seen the place in its glory
days, decades before it shut down in the seventies. We're not
sure why he never talked about that. It seemed like a pretty
remarkable story to walk around with in your back pocket.

Instead, Phil always regaled us with words of wisdom and quips
that the regulars called *Philisms*. One Philism that had since
been written on the mirror behind the bar was born when he
was simply being too nice to a boisterous customer who had
ordered a "piña colada with extra umbrellas." Phil hesitated to
throw the guy out even after the dude had broken three glasses
and a chair. Cleaning up the mess, Phil grumbled, "I need to
learn to treat people like shit. Sooner." The room erupted in
laughter, applause and chants of "Phil! Phil! Phil!"

Today, Phil's name and two dates are also scrawled on the
mirror: *Phillip Francis Krigare, Jr., 1934 - 2020*. A faded
Polaroid of him mugging with pro wrestler Jerry "The King"
Lawler is kept framed on the middle shelf, as are a busted pair
of his creepy fade-tinted bifocals.

seemed old enough to have come with the 1940s furnishings. While Phil was making the cocktail that I considered to be one of the best Old Fashioneds in all of Metro Louisville,[42] Mister Bones turned back to us and extended his hand toward me. It was tanned, had a Super Bowl-sized class ring on it, and came from the cuff of a half-rolled-up, pressed, white shirt that could have used more buttoning up.

"I'm Ronnie," he said, introducing himself.

So much of this caught me off guard. First, all the talking so far had been with Birdley, but he reached out to introduce himself to *me* first and to shake my hand before hers. I took this to be a gentlemanly courtesy; sort of a *we're-cool-man-I'm-not-hitting-on-your-girl* move. I guess I appreciated that. It's a move I have used many times to put people at ease. Dudes can be protective and territorial – especially when you're making their girlfriends laugh – and even though this move tends to momentarily disregard *her*

---

[42] An accomplishment not to be sneezed at since the cocktail was invented in Louisville at the Pendennis Club, just a hop, skip and a jump away from Sun-dried.

agency, sometimes it's best to placate the ego of any potentially stupid monkey before it grows into an angry gorilla.

The second thing that surprised me – and I'm guessing it surprised you as well! – is that he introduced himself as *Ronnie*! I guess we all thought he would be "Mister Bones" 24 hours a day.

I shook his hand which had a firm warmth that matched its tanned confidence. "Hi, I'm ███," I said, looking him in the eyes and trying to play up my role as the dude whose ego was being placated, but also trying to confidently mark my territory to equal the strength of the man-first exercise, thus deflating its effectiveness. All of my psychological handshake and eye-contact maneuvers took just a second. I'm pretty good at this shit.

Then Birdley quickly chimed up, "I'm Birdley," and reached out.

Her slender, white arm – decorated with a small, cute, flash tattoo of Lincoln's skeleton,[43] a

---

[43] You kind of have to see it. Despite having no skin or face – it doesn't even have the stovepipe hat – it's somehow obviously Lincoln.

tiny banner reading "the dogs will bark so let them bark"[44] and her wrist wrapped in a half dozen of those black, jelly loop bracelets made popular by Madonna in the eighties – was a study in contrasts to the brawny, over-bronzed grasp he put forward.

"Birdley?" he asked, chuckling a bit and carefully shaking her delicate hand. "Is that your real name?"

She had been asked *about* her name thousands of times during her 26 years, and she usually answered in a friendly way, never with even a hint of exhaustion at the question.

"No, not really," she smiled sheepishly, "but that's what everyone calls me."

"Alright, *Bird*-ley," he said, nodding in and rolling up on his toes as if to say it was all fine by him. "Nice to meet you guys."

---

[44] A line from her favorite St. Vincent song, "Birth In Reverse," *St. Vincent*, Loma Vista/Republic Records, February 24, 2014

Phil was back with our drinks and Ronnie[45] paid for everything with a flash of too much cash before we could even ask.

"I'm here alone tonight," he said, a bit quieter than all the other self-assurance he had displayed so far. Actually, he leaned in, his head between Birdley's and my ears, and said it to us like it was a secret. "Can I join you guys?"

"Sure," we both said, still fairly starstruck to hear anything in *that voice* being spoken directly to us. "We have that booth over there," I said and Birdley pointed to our favorite corner under the Bedtime Bourbon neon sign.

We made our way through the crowd and back to the booth that had been de-facto reserved by our jackets. The conversation and laughs started and continued most of the night until Vampire Motherfuckers took the stage. We all wanted to see them, including Ronnie, so we abandoned our sacred booth and stood in the steamier side room where the stage was.

---

[45] I still can't believe I get to call him Ronnie!

Birdley and I talked on the way home about how great it was that Ronnie was so easy to get along with, how cool it was that he knew some of the words to the VM's songs, and how odd it was that he was so famous yet nobody really knew what he looked like.

And really, that's how I came to be friends with Mister Bones. The three of us had a great time that first night and many more. To my surprise, he never hit on Birdley. (I know, he was maybe 35 years older than her, but maybe I just figured that that's what hot-shot people do, they take what they want. I had him all wrong. Even after Birdley left me the following year, Ronnie was a perfect gentleman, supporting me in my despair and he never said a cross word about her.)

Maybe we surprised him as well. We never asked him about his work or his on-air persona – that night or ever – which I guess might be probably rare, though I'm sure *he* knew that *we* knew by the way we acted when we first heard his voice behind me.

So what were we talking about? Oh yeah, about the author. Right. Unfortunately, *The Insider* did not take home the Oscar for Best Picture in 2000, but Scott Ritcher decided to stay in Louisville even after filming wrapped. Through early mornings and late nights, he had become friends with many of the newspaper staff he had bonded with at Abendschule and Sun-dried. Some of those friendships lasted for years. I can't say he was ever as close to any of them as I became with Ronnie, but then again, I don't know much about the author.[46]

After settling down in Kentucky, Ritcher lived for quite a few years in an apartment with mostly empty cabinets and lots of available closet space.[47] Yet he always felt he had too much. The more he

---

[46] I'm talking about Scott Ritcher, the author of *Presidential Fun Facts & Trivia*, not me, the author of *About the Author*. Because that's me.

[47] The place could use some love, but it's got good potential. And *charm!* The house has good bones. Good bones – that's what you're looking for. ... Alright, let's take a look at that back yard!

got, the less he wanted. I mean, that would be true even if the amount he wanted never changed but the number of things he had increased.

Say, for example, he wanted 20 things. So if he had 30 things, that would mean he wanted fewer things. He wanted to have 10 fewer than he had. A third of what he had, he didn't want.

Now, if he had 40 things but still wanted 20, the difference between what he had and what he wanted would be even bigger. A full 50% of all things he had would be surplus things.

So you see what I'm saying? The more he got, the less he wanted, and this was proportional and maybe exponential. Even though the amount that he wanted was always fixed at 20, the amount of space above the "wants" line and below the "has"

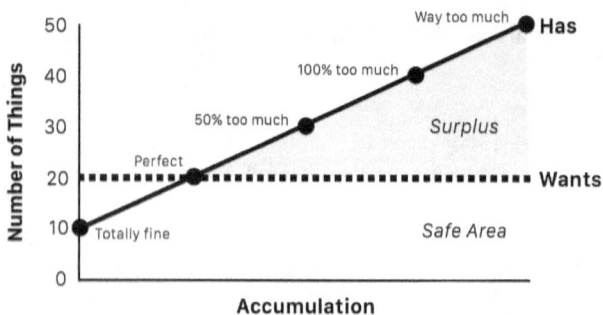

points would be proportionally larger with each new item.[48]

If there were a theme – a thread that wove through his life – it might be this: When the weather was beautiful and sunny he forgot that it had ever been any other way. But when the clouds, cold and darkness rolled in, he felt it would remain like that forever. His inner monologue was always basically the same as that of a dog who is seeing its owner either leaving the house or returning home.

Och kort sagt, pengar är lika med ångest.

Speaking of dogs, there are some cool, playful dogs in some upcoming chapters. Stay tuned.

---

[48] I don't think they were exponential. It seems like the rate of increase is constant. That is, if it isn't, in fact, slowly decreasing over time due to the fact that the baseline of *20 things* is equal to *no change* in the difference between the number of things he wanted versus the number of things he had. In that case, you could use a floating point that is proportionally equidistant from any value higher than 20. Last resort, you could steal some of his things to get him back to the number he wanted. *Which* things things to steal is a whole other issue, especially without having any knowledge of which of those things he wanted the most. Is that doobie cashed? Pass it over here, man. Where's that lighter? Thanks, man. So what were you saying?

Radium and Ether: A Love Story

For the better part of a year, Ritcher spent little time at all in his sparsely furnished abode, instead giggling and goofing around at Piper Oakley's apartment nearby.

Piper was another bespectacled charmer who found her way into his life by being funny as shit. They goaded each other incessantly and fed off each other's laughs. Inseparably but casually, they knocked around Louisville in a solid but very much undefined relationship. She could best be described as his best-friend-slash-girlfriend, and he could fit the description of comedy-muse-slash-boyfriend, though neither of them would care for those characterizations if they had a time machine and traveled here to read this book today.[49]

---

[49] Actually, I would love it if they did, just to get their opinions on the matter, and to do some other general fact checking while they're here. Although, for the record, the publisher in no way intends to provide them with free copies of the book.

Ritcher pestered her by calling her "Debbie" so
much that she came to embrace the stupidity of
the name. Piper was such a great name and he
thought it was objectively hysterical to deny her
that gift and instead give her the most uninspiring
replacement he could think of.

To show that she had warmed to the joke, she
used the name Debbie to amuse him one morning
while ordering at Coffee Exchange.[50] He nearly
collapsed in a laughter that brought him to tears.
The public disturbance of this episode so
bewildered the staff that they never forgot her
"name." On subsequent mornings, the baristas
would sometimes greet her, "Good morning,
Debbie," or simply ask, "Red Eye, Debbie?"[51]

---

[50] Coffee Exchange is on Wickenden Street in Providence. I'm not
sure why this chapter thinks it's in Old Louisville.

[51] Sometimes called a Shot in the Dark (or the Eye Opener), a
Red Eye is a cup of American-style filter coffee with a shot of
espresso in it. Other versions include the Black Eye which has
two shots of espresso and the Dead Eye which has three shots.
Piper's... I mean, *Debbie's* morning drink of choice was the
standard Red Eye. It brought her to life in the morning and
Scott knew it was working when she would grab his hand for
the first time each day or when she would make sure their legs
were touching under the table.

Ritcher introduced her as Debbie so often and to so many of his friends that many of them never knew her real name was Piper. And for the sake of clarity, we're also gonna just call her Debbie for the rest of her time in this story. And we're going call *him* Scott. It feels all too formal to call him Ritcher when talking about his time with Debbie.

Debbie's apartment was a turn-of-the-century gem in Old Louisville[52] with high ceilings, arched doorways and creaky oak floors. She had undertaken a lot of toil and expense to modernize her kitchen, one of the few places she had almost as much fun without Scott.

The only unmodern thing in the kitchen was, in fact, its centerpiece: a giant, commercial-grade gas stove with six burners and a built-in griddle. It was her altar. She had found it at an auction for under a thousand bucks, though they often sold for

---

[52] A beautiful historic-preservation district of 48 city blocks full of large, multi-story Victorian houses built beginning in the 1870s

fifteen times that. But she had spent nearly as much to have the Vulcan dismantled and reassembled in her second floor[53] apartment.

In the process of moving it in, the wall between her living room and kitchen had to be partially demolished. When she saw the light coming through both sides of the apartment at once, she liked that openness so much that she took a sledgehammer to the rest of the wall. Scott offered to help but she couldn't hear him in the madness of her glee, so he documented the obliteration spectacle in Polaroids.

Debbie put the Vulcan through its paces and finessed every bit of its heat like an orchestra conductor as she produced her

---

[53] By "second floor," the author of *About the Author* means one level up from the ground floor. Second floor (American) = first floor (European/metric).

trademark dishes: beer-soaked bratwursts,[54] spicy eggplant Parmesan and fluffy pancakes.[55] Scott devoured her cooking with same enthusiasm as he

Photograph: Debbie's 60-inch, six-burner Vulcan stove is pictured here at the auction house where she found it in West Louisville. *(Photo courtesy of Piper Oakley)*

---

[54] She and Scott were both vegetarians, but "beer-soaked *vegetarian* bratwursts" doesn't sound as good in a story. Believe me, though, any of the perfectly seasoned meals Debbie whipped up that contained meat substitutes could have fooled even the likes of Burger Reynolds, a chef.

[55] American

ate up her disrespectful jabs and the mouth they came from.

While she was composing edible symphonies in the open kitchen, he was usually laying across her green loveseat with a guitar or his small OP-1 keyboard. They would chatter and cackle across the room as they both toyed with their art. One of her go-to ribbings was the idea that she was taller than he was.[56] Debbie would make it a point to stand by his side any time she was wearing shoes[57] and he wasn't, just to stretch her length and bait him. And when he was in this loveseat with his legs dangling off the side, she would badger him by calling him "The Tower."

"Oh my God! You're *so* tall, Tower!" she would blurt over the whir of an electric mixer, then act like she couldn't hear his retort. "You're sooo

---

[56] She wasn't. Debbie was five feet, eight inches (173 cm). Scott was five feet, eleven and three quarter inches (183 cm). This was clearly an indisputable difference of three and three quarter inches (9.5 cm).

[57] Her favorite pair of red Swedish Hasbeens wooden clogs gave her an extra couple inches to work with.

much taller than I am. I mean, the Tower is, like, *dwarfing* that full-size, three-person sleeper couch!"

Of course, he fucking loved her taking the piss out of him and the Tower became as much his real name as Debbie had become hers.

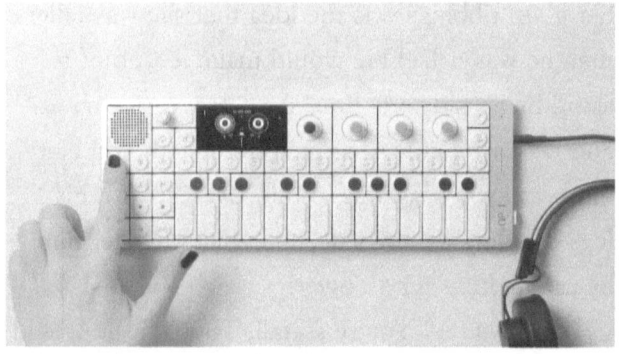

Fig. 22: The OP-1 keyboard with onboard 4-track sequencer from Teenage Engineering, like the one the Tower would play with while Debbie was working her magic in the open kitchen. Despite its small size, the device is powerful and quite expensive, regularly fetching $1,000 on eBay. If the Tower wasn't around, Debbie could always find the OP-1 on or near the vintage green loveseat in her living room. With the optional antenna accessory, it can pick up FM radio stations, so she would grab it and listen to *All Things Considered* on NPR in the afternoons while she cooked. Sampling random sounds from the radio is also a lot of fun if you feel so inclined to experiment with that. *(Photo courtesy of the manufacturer)*

Although they almost never visited the Tower's apartment, they both had keys to each other's places, and an open-door policy. She'd come home from work to find him with a mess of recording equipment set up in her apartment.[58]

"Tower, what are you doing in my apartment?"

"Shh!" He shushed her in response, "Debbie, I'm *trying* to record my podcast."

She knew his apartment was basically empty and abandoned, and she actually loved that he was in her place when she came home, but she couldn't resist starting the raillery.

"Do it at your own place," she poked.

"My place is too messy."

"Is *this* the *script*?" she snarked. "You write like a girl." And they were off to the races.

---

[58] *Here's the Tower*, episode 76, "That's So Tower," July 22, 2020, https://kcomposite.com/thats-so-tower

There's a Secret Button Under the Desk. Don't Push It.

One late summer day, they were in the apartment with the windows open. The sun was shining, the apartment was bright and a perfect breeze was blowing through, thanks to her post-demolition open floorplan. The apartment sat among the branches of tall, old maple trees on the kitchen side and oak trees on the living room side, and the breeze rustled through them all creating a wonderfully satisfying static that relaxed our protagonist and his equal half.[59]

Debbie and the Tower were both about 67% drunk after an afternoon of stacking up the Industrials.[60] Debbie was throwing together and

---

[59] They were really a team, so neither could be called the better half.

[60] An Industrial is "a beer stein filled with margarita," as detailed by Anthony Bourdain in his book, *Kitchen Confidential*, page 227, Bloomsbury Publishing, May 22, 2000.

delivering successive plates of sloppy nachos[61] in the kitchen and the Tower was noodling on the keyboard, with his legs hanging off the end of the green loveseat.

Each plate was a different variation as she was working on new approaches to this reliable dish.

Between plates, she slammed her hand on the service bell she had on her kitchen island and screamed, *"Order up for the Tower!"* then mumbled something suggestively but imperceptibly as she walked the plate over to the coffee table, sat her little butt on the armrest of the loveseat next to his head and ate the chips intentionally directly over his face.

When dispatching the third plate, she also delivered a page of the sheet music to one of his favorite pieces, *Piano Concerto No. 1 in D minor,*

---

[61] If it was up to him, he would have eaten Mexican food for every meal and the margaritas that went with it. She was also a big fan, but she could actually *make* all this stuff on a level that he could only praise. Shit, maybe she *was* the better half.

Op. 15 by Johannes Brahms.[62] She had redacted some key parts of the music and *demanded* that he figure out the missing notes from memory.

This was the type of challenge Debbie reveled in because she knew the Tower wouldn't be able to ignore it or leave it unfinished. It's like giving a kid an iPad with a really hard game on it; it will keep *them* occupied for hours and their audible and visual frustration will simultaneously entertain *you*. All he wanted to do was prove that he could do it and all she wanted was to drink more margaritas and watch his ego suffer as the mountain grew steeper.[63]

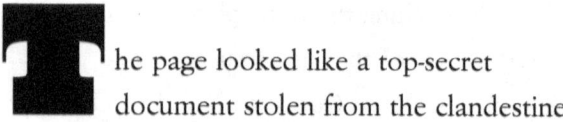he page looked like a top-secret document stolen from the clandestine

---

[62] It's one of the first musical compositions that truly slaps. A total banger.

[63] Da nerve a dis frickin' braaad!

music department at the Company,[64] with black
bars obscuring any vital information that's too
dangerous for the public's feeble minds to handle.
But aside from the sheer task of locating,
identifying and recreating the missing notes –
which might be easy enough on a grand piano –
the OP-1 keyboard is only 11 inches wide (28 cm)
and spans just two octaves. Its keys are arranged
more like a tiny typewriter's than a piano's.

In stark contrast to these two available octaves,
when Brahms composed his first piano concerto,
he splashed notes all over the fucking place. It's a
lavish spraying of notes on staffs that visually roll
up and down like whitewater rapids, but when
played, are at once dramatic and captivating like
whitewater rapids. Brahms had as much intention
of this incredible composition being condensed to
the scale of this small keyboard as the Founding
Fathers did of their words remaining unchanged

---

[64] The Company is a nickname that CIA insiders have for the
CIA, but it's generally the FBI (domestic) not the CIA
(international) that keeps tabs on musicians (Phil Ochs, John
Lennon, Whitney Houston, the Notorious BIG, Sam Cooke,
the Metroschifter, Slambang Vanilla, et al).

long after explorers had left the planet, or the American presidents did of their careers being reduced to fun facts and trivia.

The Tower *could* get the OP-1 to reach every note on the sheet, but he had to do it in swaths. First, he recorded the notes on the lowest two octaves into the keyboard. Then he'd click some buttons to raise the range of the keyboard and he'd play the notes in the next two higher octaves, adding them to the recording as it played back, and so on. All the while, he had to leave timed blank spaces in the recording sequence for the missing notes he would later recreate from memory.

Debbie had already retired for the evening and she dreamt[65] of sugarplums, butterflies and cropdusting[66] the local farmer's market while he labored on through the

---

[65] The only English root word that ends with the letters MT

[66] The act of farting while walking through a crowd of people

night. She was conked out and sawing logs by the wee hours when his task was ultimately complete.[67]

When she awoke in the following morning, she found the Tower in the living room, surrounded by bits of nachos too small to enjoy, the watery remnants of margaritas and lime slices that had been discarded as soon as the life had been sucked out of them.[68] He was wearing her oversized fuzzy cardigan (well, it was oversized on her, but it fit him perfectly), his legs were dangling off the end of the green loveseat – as they did – mouth agape, his beard decorated with a few bits of margarita-rim salt, snoring lightly in a way that sounded like a valve venting, and with the little keyboard resting on his chest as it rose and fell with his breaths.

---

[67] And, by the way, he pretty much nailed it. There were only a few misplaced notes in there, creating some diminished chords that should have been augmented. But the result probably would have sounded the same to you and other people who don't truly appreciate the genius of this piece.

[68] Foreshadowing

Before she went out the door to grab their morning fuel from Coffee Exchange, she tried to gently slide the device from under his left hand. But that movement and her poorly suppressed giggling stirred him enough that he woke up. And the first thing he consciously saw was her fingers trying to hold down all four of the T keys, a command that would erase the track.

"Oh my God you suck!" He yelled through laughs as he sprang into alertness and tried to wrestle the keyboard from her grip. She was convulsing so uncontrollably in chortles that she could no longer retain control of the device. So she threw her arms around him, squeezed hard, buried her face in his neck instead and snorted there. The wrestling spilled onto the floor and the skeletons of last night's snacks followed.

In an instant, in that explosion of elation, amusement and exhilaration, he realized he could not live without her.

It was the worst thing that could have happened to them.

It made the stakes too real, the pressure too sensitive and the repercussions of misunderstandings consequential. It made his imagination run wild in all the wrong directions. It made him always suspect the worst, when the reality was that nothing had changed. It also made this story too serious for the next few paragraphs.

As much as the Tower tried, he couldn't get small things out of his head. And they multiplied as he tried to fight them. This was the beginning of the end that had previously seemed so unimaginable.

It would have benefited him to no end if he had had a realization at this point in his life that didn't actually materialize until decades later.

The characters he created in stories like the one you're reading were compelling and appealing to him because they challenged the people around them, yet he didn't allow the people in his own life the same freedom to go outside the boundaries of what he thought was allowed for them. Contrary to what his delicate heart believed, they were, in fact, entitled to make mistakes, to do stupid things and to please themselves[69] in ways that didn't involve him. That's what made them who they were in the same way that making mistakes, doing stupid things and seeking pleasures made him who he was.

But like I said, this didn't sink in until decades later and, even then, it was a struggle for him to accept and implement this reasonable practicality.

By that time, he had long since ruined everything he and Debbie naturally had together, and she was just another distant, past stop on a long highway that stretched further than he cared to remember.

He had destroyed so many other great stops along the way as well, but Debbie truly was the *one* that got away. No, wait. Let me rephrase that: Piper Oakley was the one he should have never pushed away. He should have done everything he

---

[69] Nothing gross, just normal stuff. And before you start, we know this footnote's number is 69 and that is purely coincidental. Grow up.

could to hold on to her, but he just wasn't capable
of it at the time, so he blamed it on other things -
and other people - and forgot everything about
her that made her the perfect compliment to
everything about him.

So long, Piper. We knew you too well.

Death To the Normals

We briefly mentioned Ritcher's voluminous musical gifts earlier, but perhaps it would behoove us to discuss his music career[70] in greater detail.

That same year (this year, I think), Ritcher's music group (the) Metroschifter[71] won a Grammy[72] for their record *Strawberries*. What a great record. They really knocked it out of the park with that one.

The following year (the one before this one but after the last one), Ritcher added a gold record[73]

---

[70] That's a generous way to put it.

[71] This part is true.

[72] This part is not true.

[73] A single or album that achieves sales of more than 500,000 copies in the United States as verified by the Recording Industry Association of America. All of Ritcher's records *combined* are as far from this milestone as William Howard Taft is from being included in a book of fun facts and trivia, this footnote notwithstanding.

to his extensive hall of trophies[74] in 2019 for his groundbreaking[75] record *The Kentuckian*. Again, wow.

It's weird to think that there had been a point in his life, when he was 21, where he almost chose film over music. Ritcher's music career[76] has been dogged by criticism of his inability to sing *properly* and being a filmmaker generally requires no singing talent whatsoever. Bergman, Hitchcock, Welles, that other one; none of them had a solo acoustic act.

So regardless of whether he would have been a better filmmaker than he was a musician, I'll have to say it, and I think most people would agree, that for someone who couldn't sing, he did alright for himself.

---

[74] If I recall correctly, the only trophy he ever won was for the Pinewood Derby. The prize for the Lego-building contest he won (more about that coming up later in the book) was just more Legos.

[75] Come on, man.

[76] Again with this one?

Wi-Fi Sickness

A t age 66, like he needed more adoration, all the late nights Scott Ritcher had spent toiling in his drafty, candlelit laboratory finally began to pay off.

It was in the autumn of 2008 that he discovered both the origin and cause of Wi-Fi Sickness,[77] was awarded the Nobel Prize for Burritos and hosted the sixth season of television's *Animal Autopsy*. It was a busy autumn.

These high-profile accomplishments and their accompanying acclaim caught the eye of a young chess prodigy and amateur police detective. The future Mrs. Scott Ritcher went out of her way to get noticed. And it worked. He took her to be his third wife. Her name was Mrs. Scott Ritcher.

His bride was both stunning and cute, with icy blue eyes, dark black hair, light freckles on her

---

[77] It was Wi-Fi.

nose and cheeks, and eyelashes that were always
clumped together. She infamously had no buffer
between her pretty little head and her filthy
fucking mouth.

A totally different and more volatile flavor than
Debbie, this broad was certifiably nuts and you
could smell the crazy on her a mile away.[78]

r. Ritcher wavered between flustered
and charmed by her many
idiosyncrasies.

In text messages, she would sometimes reply
with an asterisk and correct the grammar in the
messages other people had sent to her. The
national chess federation repeatedly fined her for
groaning, "Oh, suck my dick," when her
opponents scored advantages during professional-
level matches. In restaurants, she took plates away
from overweight strangers, telling them, "You've
had just about enough." She looked up Mensa

---

[78] Roughly 1.61 kilometers away

meetings in the area, just to sit outside and play the drums on empty buckets – and it was always *that one* drumbeat that girl drummers play in punk bands, you know, the one where it's like they think the floor tom is the hi-hat.[79] She obsessively hunted down and hoarded what was perhaps the world's largest private collection of Obama fan fiction, even commissioning new stories from writers on gig sites like Fiverr. She shoved the doorman at a Chicago hotel, saying, "Outta the way, virgin." Her favorite mix tape was a compilation of just the really high note parts of Mariah Carey songs. She simply *adored* ruining people's birthdays.

The couple constantly tested each other's patience and blood pressure limits by hiding behind doors or walls in the house and screaming as the other one walked in. They both *hated it* when the other person did it, but they both loved doing it. Well, actually, they only hated it for the first few seconds after the initial blast of fright, but typically laughed with a cross look, a shaking head

---

[79] It's not.

and a pointed finger once the bloodcurdling screams subsided. One particular wall in the house, on the dining room side of the kitchen door, was so damaged by coffee stains as the result of terror jolts that they eventually painted it dark brown.

As Scott[80] began to expect her to be hiding behind the dining room door, he would enter quietly in an attempt to preemptively scare her instead. It happened more than once that she was hiding next to the wall on the other side of the door – behind him in this case – so she successfully scared the living shit out of him anyway.

Exhibit 39: Mrs. Scott Ritcher's mix tape marked "Mariah Carey Squeals." It was just the high-voice singing parts over and over.

---

[80] We're calling him Scott in this part of the story because they both shared the surname Ritcher after their wedding.

Goddammit, Honey, the Firmament and the Sky Are the Same Thing

Their back-and-forth bullying was somewhat uproarious. It appeared to be good natured fun from the outside, but something more was happening beneath the surface. It was taking a psychological toll on the pair.

Larger cracks[81] began to appear in the couple's moderately tolerable bond during a late night conversation over what they might name their children, in the event that they should produce human offspring. After they agreed on a few great names – Friday Yolo was a popular choice, as was Emmma with three M's – she suggested the name Hailey.

He exploded, "That's a *murder victim's* name!"

"What?" she offered hesitantly, "I kinda like it."

---

[81] Cracks. Uh huh huh huh huh huh.

98

"You want our kid to get *murdered?*" he protested.

Flustered, she said, "We don't *have* a kid! You can't murder someone who doesn't exist."

"I didn't say *I* was going to murder it," he said.

"You said it can't get murdered because it doesn't exist," she blurted.

"*You* said that, not me!"

"Correlation is not causation, dude! Just because something exists doesn't mean that it causes things to happen."

He sat with a confused look on his face, trying desperately to understand what the hell she meant. "So just because our kid exists... which it doesn't... that causes it to get killed?"

"Yes! It doesn't matter what we name it. Hailey or whatever else," she paused and dug herself in, visibly corncobbing[82] at this point. "And obviously I know *you* wouldn't kill our kid. You can't even murder a spider, you fucking pussy."

---

[82] Having lost an argument but continuing to dig yourself in deeper and in complete denial of the loss, thereby destroying any credibility or validity that you or your argument might have had

The jabs and logic devolved from there, and when these spats became more frequent - including repeated discussions about whether paper towels or electric hand dryers were better for the environment[83] - the couple began to drift apart.

Another straw that added more weight to the camel's back in their heated relationship was apparently the fact that she always left the toilet seat up. I'm not sure why she did that or how that even worked. (Did she straddle the toilet? Hover above it? Was she sitting on the bare rim? I certainly can't imagine that she was standing.)

Sadly, although the toilet seat thing became a bit of an impasse, fate did not allow their romance sufficient time to fully disintegrate.

---

[83] The publisher is not at liberty to disclose the answer.

In July,[84] Mrs. Scott Ritcher inadvertently wandered into range of a password-protected high-speed internet signal and was stricken with a nasty bout of Wi-Fi Sickness.[85]

She stumbled about like a sweaty boob for several days before finding cool refuge in the shade of an old mulberry tree, or some kind of other tree. I don't know tree types.[86] A gust of wind loosened a heavy branch that fell from high in the tree, crackling on its way down, until it bonked her plum square on the noggin with a force sufficient enough to send her post-haste to an untimely demise.

---

[84] There's no known way of saying an English sentence in which you begin a sentence with "in" and emphasize it. Get me a jury and show me how you can say "*In* July" and I'll go down on you. That's just idiotic, if you forgive me by saying so. That's just stupid. "*In* July"? I'd love to know how you emphasize "in" in "In July." Impossible! Meaningless!

[85] How many more lives must be destroyed before people start leaving their networks open?

[86] I know we talked about maple and oak trees earlier in the book, but I only knew what those trees were because someone told me. That's actually where I got the idea to call this one a mulberry. I know it was a big tree, but I already used oak and maple. Mulberry is another type of tree that I have heard of.

Mrs. Scott Ritcher's funeral was an emotional affair. Most funerals are emotional affairs. Those emotions tend to be sad ones.

In the months after her dirt nap commenced, the man she left behind (Scott Ritcher) took to leaving the toilet seat up himself to honor her memory in his own pathetic way. What a loser.[87]

Ritcher slept late into his days and did irresponsible things like you might have read about in other books about other people who experienced similar losses. He quite honestly couldn't stand her while she was alive, but not having her around was somehow worse. Without her, paper towels and hand dryers became all the

---

[87] You know, a lot of people are saying he's a loser, and a lot of people are saying many things about him. I don't know if it's true, if any of it is true, but there are many people who think that he's a loser. A total loser, quite frankly. I don't bring it up because I don't know enough to really discuss it. I will say there are people who continue to bring it up because they think he is absolutely a loser. I don't do that because I don't think it's fair. But we're going to look at that and plenty of other things. Believe me.

same to him. He was both fragile and useless, like a bag of dead lightbulbs. He was at sixes and sevens, as much a door as he was a window.

No surprise, then, that Ritcher's little, broken heart was nearly available and all but ripe for the picking when he was wooed by Hollywood actress Kirsten Dunst.[88]

---

[88] Nominated for Best Supporting Actress, *The Power of the Dog*, Academy Awards, 2022. Winner for Best Actress, *Melancholia*, Cannes Film Festival, 2011. Nominated for four Golden Globe Awards for acting: *Interview with the Vampire*, 1995; *Fargo*, 2016; *On Becoming a God In Central Florida*, 2020; *The Power of the Dog*, 2022.

Sex, Drugs and Politics

He had always been the target of starlets. He was so good looking and charming, they couldn't resist him. It must have been exhausting, am I right?

Dunst had a curious way of courting, all the way up to when she proposed to him by saying she was asking for a friend. He found this particular shenanigan to be satisfying, and as he was so disposed, they were wed in a private ceremony in 1992.

The ceremony was not held at the White House (as it had been for President Grover Cleveland and Frances Folsom some 106 years earlier), but at Dunst's makeshift campaign headquarters in Lexington, the year before she won the Kentucky gubernatorial election. She also became governor of Kentucky around that same time. After, I think.

Ritcher's years with Kiki in the Governor's Mansion were filled with glitz, gallantry and probably another word that starts with G, but I can't really think of one.

The glamour of life in Montpellier, Kentucky's capital,[89] was also a period of warmth for the couple. They were often seen playing on the front lawn with their mischievous dogs, Pockets and Unsubscribe. They hosted a weekly audiobook club at the mansion. They giggled like school kids whenever they could to slip the word "panties" into a sentence.

As a show of goodwill, they made a habit of welcoming everyone to the Governor's Mansion, regardless of political persuasion. At a ceremony honoring Eugene Cernan,[90] even Kiki's political rivals were offered pizza bites and cautioned not to burn the roofs of their mouths.[91]

---

[89] Not Kentucky's capital

[90] The last man to walk on the Moon as of press time

[91] According to philosopher Alice Löfgren, that part of the body should be called the *ceiling* of the mouth. A roof is on the outside of something and the mouth doesn't have an outside.

The Rebel In Me Lives Again

The magic of living the Governor's Mansion seemed to be but a passing respite from a larger darkness as Ritcher slowly descended into waking up at the crack of noon, day drinking,[92] the frequent smoking of reefer doobies and all sorts of other awesome shit. I'd be surprised if you've even heard of half the stuff he was rolling in.

---

[92] At this point, his go-to cocktail was known as the Party Starter. In a rocks glass, muddle 2 pieces of Ferrero Pocket Coffee, mix in 2 shots of espresso, 2 shots of Evan Williams Bottled-In-Bond Bourbon and 2 dashes of El Yucateco Green Habanero Sauce. Drop in 1 home-size ice cube and fill the rest of the glass with Founder's KBS bourbon barrel-aged chocolate coffee stout. (You'll have some KBS left over.) Stir, then pour the entire contents of the glass into a camping thermos. (Careful, now, with those last steps on account of the KBS which might take a liking to fizzing up a bit.) Enjoy, but for the love of God, please drink responsibly.

In the rare event that all those ingredients were not readily available, his second choice was the Industrial (see footnote 60 on page 80) though it tended to remind him of Debbie.

These are lemon trees on a California ranch where lemons are grown. You can't really see the lemons in this photo, but despite that and the author's lack of knowledge about tree types, the publisher assures you that these are lemon trees. See footnote 86 on page 100, footnote 93 on page 107.

As time wore on, it became clear to the Governor that Ritcher's mastery of the kissing arts simply wasn't enough to justify keeping him around. The risk of irreversible political liability was getting far too likely for her. So, shortly after he handed out glow sticks at a formal state dinner, she, too, grew tired of his antics. At this point, even I am tired of his antics.

The couple remained married purely for the sake of keeping up appearances, but Ritcher was cast from the Governor's Mansion and sent to work in exile on a lemon ranch in Yorba Linda, California. It was the poorest lemon ranch in California, I can assure you.

Picking lemons was hard work, but he enjoyed joking around with the other lemon pickers and discussing all manner of popular culture. He learned quite a bit from them about keeping the trees[93] happy so they would grow juicier lemons. He also found the citrus aroma to be more to his liking than parts of rural Kentucky which had a tendency to smell a lot more like... let's say, um, agriculture. I think you know what I mean. And if you don't, you should maybe get out more often.

---

[93] When I said I didn't know tree types, I guess I wasn't thinking about lemon trees. They're more obvious than, say, oak or elm trees. I know lemon trees. Orange trees, too. That's easy.

About the Author's Dogs

While working himself ridiculous on the lemon ranch, as was expected, Ritcher missed the Bluegrass State and the social status he had left behind. He was also overcome with the general feeling that he had squandered what could have been more idyllic times with Kiki in the Governor's Mansion.

He longed for the companionship of the couple's two dogs, Pockets and Unsubscribe, who had stayed behind in Kentucky.

Pockets, a Siberian husky with heterochromia iridum,[94] was named for his tendency as a puppy to collect things and hoard them in a small corner

---

[94] Heterochromia iridum is the condition of having two different colored eyes, like Ritcher's former lover, Hollywood actress Kate Bosworth (star of the Netflix thriller series *The I-Land* which earned an average Tomatometer score of 8%). In Pockets' case, it was one icy blue eye and one light brown eye.

Pockets waiting to go for a run on the grounds of the Governor's Mansion; age 4 ½ in human years

Unsubscribe in a winter sweater and a rare moment of composure; age 19 in dog years

of the living room. This habit continued as Pockets grew to the size of a small wolf. His wolflike appearance and size could be a bit unsettling to strangers, but he quickly compensated for it by being the sweetest, most respectful dog you'd ever have the honor to share a sofa, a blanket, a book and an afternoon with.

Unsubscribe had also earned her name when she was a puppy, and that name was also based on her personality. She was a rambunctious and indefatigable Boston Terrier who wanted to play pretty much every single hour of the day. The Governor, in a fit of exasperation while working on a speech, blurted at the eager black and white dog, "Enough! *Unsubscribe already!*" When that outburst got an immediate snort-style laugh from Scott, the dog was as good as named.

For as annoying as Unsubscribe could be, she was just as easily Scott's little darling. Her asymmetrical cow-style spots accented her little face in a yin-yang fashion, the black area covering the right half with a great white splash that fell from between her ears, down the left-center of her forehead and wrapped around her nose. The nose itself was black, as were her tiny lips and a smudge between her nose and mouth.

With the exception of the dogs' tongues and Pockets' eyes, these two companions looked very much the same in black and white photos as they did in person. (The black and white at play on Pockets' wolflike face was much more angular, striped and exciting, circling his eyes like finger glasses.)

Unsubscribe was just as enamored with Scott as he was with her. He often dressed her in a scarf or bandana, or a little sweater, depending on the season. She relished the attention of outfit changes and seemed to jump right into whatever he leaned down to put on her, then she'd bounce around the room as if showing off her new style.

This is not to say that Unsubscribe was the favorite. Ritcher and the Governor doted on both dogs and talked to them in a matter-of-fact way as if they were humans, never condescending to baby talk. But this reporter was particularly taken with Unsubscribe the first time I interviewed the couple at their apartment in Nashville, Kentucky's largest city.[95]

Pockets was known to fart so thunderously in his sleep that he would wake up in fear. Not much could be done about the condition, medically, that is. However, seeing it happen, though, was priceless.

---

[95] Not in Kentucky

From the outset, Pockets had cost $750, a fair price for an animal of this quality and aplomb.

Unsubscribe had been a bit more expensive at $900, yet still quite a good deal for the level of energy and joy she brought to all who encountered her.

Within the context of a story about these two lovable companions, perhaps you find a discussion of their cost to be a bit distasteful. I understand that. However, for the purposes of tax records (and other things that we can't talk about yet because they would include some pretty unsatisfying spoilers), the publisher would like to make it clear that Mr. Ritcher was not reimbursed by the Governor when he paid a combined $1,650 for the two dogs, plus Kentucky state sales tax of 6%, bringing the grand total to $1,749 in 1992 (roughly equivalent to $3,781 in 2023). Also, it seems like this should have been a footnote instead of being included as part of the story. But whatever. Write your own book.

Freudian Emoji

As Ritcher entered his 60s (again) and the degree of his physical asymmetry increased, he became quite adept at hitting his head on stuff while leaning over to pick things up. Be it a rogue slice of carrot or a bottle cap on the kitchen floor that drew his attention, the counter-top was always there to greet his forehead on the way down, and an open cabinet door would caress the back of his noodle as he rose again.

It was during this comically injurious period that he began work on his influential and seminal work *Presidential Fun Facts & Trivia*, the award-winning[96] tome you hold now in your hands. Maybe you're holding in one hand. It's pretty small, really. (The book is small, not your hand. I'm sure you have *very* normal sized hands.)

---

[96] What's that big book prize called? I think that's one of the ones it won. It certainly won one.

PINECONE CINEMAS 8

CHECK TIMES DAILY
DOLBY STEREO = ★

$3.50 MON-FRI ALL SHOWS BEFORE 6 P.M.
SAT, SUN & HOLIDAYS 1st MATINEE ONLY

1426 O.J. SIMPSON BLVD, D'TOWN
ACROSS FROM SUNDRIED FACTORY

MONDAY-WEDNESDAY

JURASSIC PARK (PG) ★
127 min.
10:00a 1:30p 4:00p 6:30p 9:00p 11:30p
Two paleontologists and an eccentric mathematician tour an island theme park populated by dinosaurs created from prehistoric DNA. The park's billionaire owner assures everyone the facility is safe, but when ferocious predators break free, chaos ensues and the group is cast into a fight for survival.
• Sam Neill, Laura Dern, Jeff Goldblum, Richard Attenborough; Dir: Steven Spielberg

THE INSIDER (PG) ★
157 min.
10:00a 1:30p 4:00p 6:30p 9:00p 11:30p
A seasoned TV news producer persuades a former tobacco exec to share his knowledge of industry secrets, but suspects there is something behind his reluctance to speak. And a handsome newspaper photographer stands in the background while someone talks on the phone.
• Scott Ritcher, Russell Crowe, Al Pacino; Dir: Michael Mann; No passes

THURSDAY

JURASSIC PARK (PG) ★
127 min.
10:00a 1:30p 4:00p 6:30p 9:00p 11:30p
Two fucking kids annoy a genius who is trying to figure all this out while some lady buries her entire arm in a pile of dinosaur shit. Nature finds a way and Col. Sanders yells at Newman.

FRIDAY-SATURDAY

JURASSIC PARK (PG) ★
127 min.
10:00a 1:30p 4:00p 6:30p 9:00p 11:30p
A misunderstood visionary copes with administrative issues and electrical problems while launching an innovative theme park.

AVBLIN AND THE CHIPCHUNKS (R)
94 min.
11:00a 12:45p 3:30p 7:30p 10:45p
After the tree they call home is shipped to LA, three insufferable talking chipmunks meet a manipulative songwriter who sells them to a record company. Contains nudity.
• Merle Haggard, Emmma Ritcher-Fjällltorp, Friday Yolo Ritcher; Dir: Ingmar Begrman

SALEM WITCH TRIALS EXPOSED (R)
99 min
1:45p 4:00p 6:00p 8:15p
Investigative documentary journalist reveals evidence that many witches were rightfully executed and argues that several more witches escaped prosecution through trickery.
• Dir: Armond Pastore; No masturbating

SUNDAY

SPECIAL EVENT: MEET AUTHOR SCOTT RITCHER IN PERSON
3:00p
Presidential trivia expert and host of TV's "Animal Autopsy" in live Q&A with WTWR-FM jock Mister Bones; 90 min., 18+, No passes

Many intellectuals and academics postulate that exploration of the presidents might never be complete, and yet *Presidential Fun Facts & Trivia* challenges that very notion. This expansive volume conveys virtually every nuance one might require to understand the history of the presidency and, yes, in turn, life itself.

What can one say about this historic landmark of a book that hasn't yet been said by critic and fan alike? Whose parents and grandparents haven't a dusty vintage edition of *Presidential Fun Facts & Trivia* tucked away on an unremarkable shelf, surrounded by the lesser works of Faulkner and that other lady? What is a library?

And yet throughout Ritcher's life – a life bedazzled with triumphs (at a young age he brutally crushed the competition in a Lego building contest[97] at Louisville's Oxmoor mall),

---

[97] His prize-winning entry was a spectacular model of Walt Disney World's Contemporary Resort Hotel in Orlando, Florida, complete with monorail.

and scarred by tragedy (he was once charged 70 euros[98] by Scandinavian Airlines just to take his guitar from Berlin to Stockholm. It's not that far and, honestly, if it's that much for a guitar, how much did they charge for that screaming baby to ruin that same flight for *all* their customers?) – he rarely acted as if he was even aware of the historic scale of his achievements in the world of presidential trivia.

Some say it was the repeated luggage surcharges that finally did him in at the end of his incredibly long and stupid life.

Others speculate it was the compounding aggravation of seeing strangers repeatedly cough and sneeze into their hands that weakened his resolve. "In your *hand?!*" he would grumble at them, "You touch everything with that hand."[99]

We may never know.

---

[98] A different amount in regular money

[99] *Here's the Tower*, episode 67, "Everything You Touched," May 20, 2020
https://kcomposite.com/everything-you-touched

Regardless of which petty nonsense caused him to ultimately meet his demise, it is with great pride that Mr. Ritcher must be looking down on us now today from his high horse[100] with whom he was laid to rest[101] in 1980-something.

---

[100] This is the only mention of horses in this book and it is a figurative horse. (This disclaimer does not include the mention of the Kentucky Derby on page 56. Yes, that is a horse race, but horses were not explicitly mentioned in the text.)

[101] He ain't dead yet.

Too Old to Make Out

On a chilly, overcast Monday morning in October 1981, Scott Ritcher's friends and family joined celebrities and dignitaries from around the world to pay their respects to one of the nation's most respected authors, thinkers and experts in presidential fun facts.

It was on this day that Ritcher would be laid to rest at Sleepytime Acres, a sparse, rustic cemetery, dotted with unreadable headstones whose names and edges had long since been rounded off by the elements, speckled by mold, caressed by moss, kissed for centuries by each morning's dew and baked by each afternoon's glow.

Struggling against the bite of the unseasonably cold air[102] that whipped across this rural Kentucky

---

[102] It had blown in earlier the previous evening with a low-pressure front from the northwest. Overcast skies were expected with a high around 46° Fahrenheit (that's 7.8° Celsius, or the adjective *inferior*).

hillside, Hollywood actress Claire Foy and Hollywood actress Riley Keough clutched hands tightly as they mourned their loss, their knuckles turning white-purple under the pressure of this desperate grip and the unforgiving chill in the air. Occasionally sharing a knowing glance with Hollywood actress Lizzy Caplan who stood alone, shivering gently on the opposite side of Ritcher's flag-draped[103] coffin, the Hollywood actresses tried to offer reassuring smiles through their sobs.

A number of Sir Ritcher's non-celebrity former lovers and associates joined them in their grief. His once indispensable companion Piper "Debbie" Oakley was solemn, a nearly unrecognizable version of the wide-eyed, bursting character she had been by his side. His former wife, Mrs. Scott Ritcher donned an understated black dress with a white Peter Pan collar; her lips a somber, deep

---

[103] It was a green flag from a discount electronics store emblazoned with the words "We beat any price" in Gill Sans Bold, an overused and controversial font. (Scott Ritcher, "Fontroversy," *Snuggling With the Enemy*, October 2009, https://sweden.kcomposite.com/fontroversy)

red; her freckles muted by white powder and the season.

And although they had been out of touch for decades, Annabel van de Velde quietly made the trip away from her family in Brussels to pay her respects. She had married a successful businessman in haste, not long after her whirlwind romance with Ritcher had fallen apart. While he had been drowning his sorrows at sea aboard the *Columbia*, she became despondent in the belief that he was ignoring her calls and letters. Almost as an act of spite, she fell into a comfortable life with a self-made frites-shack[104] magnate to mask her lovesick despair. Though the couple had two beautiful twins,[105] a spacious loft in Antwerp[106] and by all appearances seemed to live an idyllic life, Annabel had never truly loved the businessman and she

---

[104] Belgian french fries that come in a paper cone, sold in street kiosks with your choice of dipping sauce

[105] Two twins total, not two sets of twins. There was one boy and one girl. They were not identical. Obviously. The girl, who had those same milky tan skin and reddish brown hair as her mother, was already well on her way to becoming the same type of carefree whirlwind that played fast and loose with life.

[106] The biggest city in Belgium

longed for the days when her skin was flawless, flowing softly over her unforgettable clavicles, warmed by the sun, his lips, and brushed by her loose braids. In short, she had always regretted letting the fire with Ritcher burn out so carelessly. She cursed that immature version of herself, but she couldn't go back.[107] After letting him go, she had just played along with what life thought she was supposed to do.

Annabel was overcome with memories and physically crippled in pain as a touching remembrance was read by Hollywood actress Sienna Miller.

What would any of us here today know about the presidents," she asked, "had not been for our time with Li'l Scotty?" She referred to him using one of the

---

[107] Time travel was still not possible in the 1980s unless you landed there from a later time. But an originating departure was not possible.

nicknames she had liked to call him before he got all dead and stuff.

"How many presidential facts... fun or otherwise... could we have counted among us?"

Just a few sentences in, there was nary a dry eye on the hillside, and Miss Miller trembled as she bravely powered on.

"What some call trivia," she paused, "I call love." And with that, Hollywood actress and two-time Primetime Emmy Award[108] winner Claire Foy began audibly bawling her fucking eyes out, for she had also lost much more than just a great resource for presidential trivia. She had lost the most sensitive man and compassionate lover she suspected she might ever know.

---

[108] Outstanding Lead Actress in a Drama Series, *The Crown*, 2018 & 2021

Off to one side, seemingly unnoticed in this sea of celebrity,[109] silently stood Robyn Fenty, the stunning Barbadian singer and businesswoman known to the world as Rihanna.[110] She had been enamored by the liberties Ritcher had taken when he interpreted her songs (back when he was alive, of course) and she once told a reporter, "I consider my endless string of global hit records to be sort of like the demos for the brilliance he brought to the songs. In his hands, they got real meaning."

Rihanna's angular, wraparound, jet black rain coat cut an impressive silhouette against the grey sky. The solid shape of this dark color was interrupted only by a tiny, weathered locket hanging on a thin, silver chain. Her understated makeup revealed a naturally soft honesty that she seldomly bared for the public. But this day was different for her as well.

---

[109] Well, mostly celebrities, but also lots of really cool goth and punk chicks

[110] Appointed to the Barbados Order of National Heroes, 2018

Inside that locket was a photo of her and Scott on the beach together, their eyes shining brightly under the effects of the recreational drug ecstasy,[111] on a night that inspired her 2012 hit "Diamonds."

Miss Miller continued, her voice growing weaker, "*He* taught us that some facts about the presidents are fun." She wiped a tear from her cheek, "While other information about the presidents is trivial."

Hollywood actress Claire Danes wavered at those words, but coolly regained her balance.

---

[111] Street name for MDMA or 3,4-Methyl enedioxy methamphetamine, also known as molly

As Hollywood actress Sienna Miller concluded her heartfelt eulogy, a hush fell over the crowd of mostly hotties.[112] An unexpected murmur grew and heads slowly turned, as a black stretch limousine slowed to a stop on the damp, gravel, one-lane road nearby. The engine was cut and after a few brief seconds that felt longer than regular seconds, the rear, starboard-side door slowly opened. An elegant foot emerged from below the door, stepping onto the gravel driveway, decisively, in a very smart black boot. (I would tell you the brand, but you've probably never heard of it and you certainly could never afford it.)

And at once, there she was.

---

[112] Some pretty solid 8's and, I mean, I don't think I'm going out on a limb saying there were a couple of killer 9's. Keough and Foy, am I right? And I think that might be Janelle Monáe over there. Yes, Hollywood actress Janelle Monáe. Yeah, the one in the hat. Don't stare.

The celebrated Hollywood actress and former two-term governor of the Commonwealth of Kentucky, Kirsten Caroline Dunst Ritcher[113] rose from behind the dark window.

A translucent black veil masked her sorrow. An even darker knee-length wool coat protected her from the cold. But this coat also shielded prying eyes from a small baby bump. Yes, to this rural funeral she was carrying not only a heart full of sadness, but also the unborn eleventh child of one of America's greatest living authors.[114]

Pockets and Unsubscribe hopped down and out of the car behind her, off leash, but much slower now in their old age, their black spots licked by gray. Even they seemed to sense that something was missing from the universe. (Well, dogs can smell everything, so it wasn't so much a *sense* that

---

[113] She kept his name long after they split, for it had become an indispensable element of her personal brand, both politically and culturally.

[114] "Living?" What the... He's in that coffin about to get buried! If he's still alive, somebody should really say something.

something was missing, as much as it was their senses of smell.[115] They knew their former human was dead and in that box over there.[116])

As she quietly approached, the mourning congregation had begun tossing flowers on the coffin, touching it gently and saying their last goodbyes. Inside that mahogany sarcophagus were several cubic feet of unfinished dreams, lost passions, at least a few more presidential facts, some of them fun, and, yes, perhaps a bit of trivia.

Shaking, Governor Dunst slowly placed her delicate right hand on the cold casket. In her left hand, she held tightly to a first-edition copy of *Presidential Fun Facts & Trivia,* just like the one you're holding in your hands right now. Her treasured paperback had been autographed inside the back pages by Ritcher, her favorite former

---

[115] Triumph the Insult Comic Dog, "Sense of Smell," *Come Poop With Me*, Warner Bros. Records, November 4, 2003

[116] Oh. So he *is* dead?

husband, lover, confidant, lover, soulmate and lover. It also had a number of handwritten notes and souvenir stickers in it.

Against all silence but for the wind, she spoke softly.

This book," she said as the quiet drew closer and her voice – part eloquence, part announcement – echoed off the bluegrass hillside, "meant everything to him."

Hollywood actress Lizzy Caplan's knees buckled, and though Jared from Subway[117] rushed to help stabilize her, she brushed him away in Melanian fashion.

"He may be gone," Kiki continued, "but *this* gift he gave us will live on. For it is we, the educated elite, who hold his research dear."

At this moment, a sliver of sunlight peeked through the clouds, bounced off the shiny coffin and illuminated her veiled face. Kiki pulled back

---

[117] Not real sure why he was there, but okay

the veil, revealing her flawless, pale skin, a path of teardrops and mascara drawn down her cheeks, and on her neck, a freshly inked *Presidential Fun Facts & Trivia* tattoo, still taped under its plastic wrap.

"It is we who keep his legacy alive each time we crack open the pages of this trusty volume," her voice rose with her arm as she held the tattered book aloft.

"I don't know much about the presidents," she confessed, which drew a few chuckles of agreement, for many of these gorgeous funeral guests were also limited in their knowledge of the presidents. "But what I *do* know, is that Grover Cleveland was the only president to be wed in office."

With that, several of the smokin' hot mourners pursed their lips and nodded their heads. "Yes," whispered Hollywood actress Riley Keough, "So true... so true."

But the former governor wasn't finished. The congregation hung on her every word.

"And I *also* know," she sniffled, "that Cleveland's marriage ceremony with Frances Folsom," she paused, "was held at the White House. In June of 1886."

The silence was deafening. Everyone knew she was right. What had just moments ago been a sad remembrance had suddenly turned hopeful and appreciative.

"And I know *that*... because of *this man*... right here," Kiki said, gently pounding her fist on the casket. "This man... right here."

The nods and tears in the crowd gave way to half smiles as she concluded.

"May he sleep so softly with the angels this night."[118]

---

[118] Again, seriously, I don't think he's dead yet.

Extra fluffy
American pancakes

If you like American pancakes[119] – and you'd have to be a damn fool not to – you'll be delighted to know how simple it is to whip up one of Piper Oakley's[120] go-to specialties on the weekend morning of your choice.

What you'll need

Metric	Ingredient	Imperial[121]
210 grams	all-purpose flour	1 ½ cups
10 ml	baking powder	2 teaspoons
50 grams	granulated sugar	¼ cup
2 large	eggs	3 large
55 grams	melted butter	¼ cup
240 ml	milk	1 cup
1 pinch	salt	1 pinch
Some	vegetable oil	Some
More	butter for cooking	More

You can add 10 ml (2 teaspoons) of vanilla extract for a little extra cozy flavor if you like... *I like!* [122]

---

[119] Commonly known as "pancakes"

[120] Commonly known as "Debbie"

[121] Commonly known as "regular"

[122] Really? You're still doing Borat?

1 In a big bowl, whisk the flour, sugar, salt and baking powder together. We will refer to this mix as *the dry stuff*.

2 Separately, in another bowl, mix the eggs, melted butter and milk. We will refer to this mix as *the wet stuff*. If you are using vanilla extract, add it to this wet mix.

I know it sounds crazy to create these wet and dry mixes separately since you're eventually going to mix them all together, but trust me, it makes a difference. If you don't believe me, just go ahead and do it your own way and see what happens. I'll wait.

Another thing that might sound crazy to Americans and Europeans alike is that eggs come in boxes of ten in most of Europe, but in America, eggs come in dozens, because of course they do.

Keep this in mind while doing your grocery shopping.

5 This is the part where the two mixes become one.[123] Grab that whisk and mix your wet stuff and your dry stuff together into one mix. If it's big enough, you can use one of the bowls that one of the mixes is already in and just fold in the stuff from the other bowl.

When that mix is all smooth, thick and free of lumps, your pancake batter is ready!

This is a special moment and you can treat yourself by having a little taste of the batter. Wash your hands first. You really should have washed your hands before you started all this. Sicko.

4 Heat up your pancake griddle to a medium heat. Don't be afraid to make it

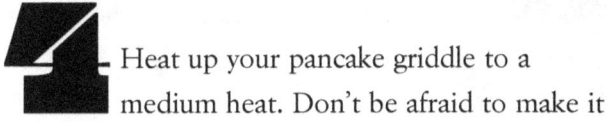

hot, but don't go too hot. And this is key: *let it get hot and stay hot for a while.*

An especially important rule in the world of pancakes is that a freshly heated surface is not the same as a surface that has been hot for a while. It's like kissing. The first contact is exciting, but it's so much more fun after you've been in there for a while and your whole body is a part of it. You're old enough now that I shouldn't have to explain this to you. But if you still don't get it, come over sometime and I can show you.

If you don't have a proper, flat pancake griddle because you're poor or divorced or some other kind of loser,[124] you can use a non-stick frying pan.

5 Drop a slice of butter and a spoonful of vegetable oil in the middle of the griddle and let it heat up. It'll look frothy when it's ready.

---

[124] Get your shit together. Stop feeling sorry for yourself. Get a job, turkey.

6 Pour in some of the batter to make your first pancake. The batter will grow in surface area and height as it heats up, so watch yourself. Now, if them cakes is too close together, they's liable to grow into each other. That'd give ya one big, messy pancake in a funny shape.

If that's what you want, fine. I'm not gonna tell you how to live your life. But if you want some classic, beautiful pancakes that look like a gorgeous photo in a cookbook or like the pancake emoji,[125] which also appears in *this* book (at the bottom of this page), you'll want to make sure you have enough space between them cakes. I know you probably can't afford an industrial stove with a built-in griddle,[126] but the bigger your griddle, the better. Give yourself enough room to make your art. Glenn Gould wasn't fucking around on a Casio. The Dutch Masters weren't doodling on postcards. Well, Rembrandt maybe, but then he got serious about his art, and you should, too.

---

[125]

[126] Like a 60-inch Vulcan, for example

7 Let the first side of the pancakes cook for a minute or two until you see lots of small bubbles forming and they start popping on the surface. The cakes should be golden brown on the underside when you lift up an edge with a spatula. This is when you need to flip 'em.

Bring your A-game. Don't hesitate. Quickly slip that spatula under that pancake and lift it up. Don't go too high when you've got it in the air. Move it to the side and flip it down like you're closing the back cover of a hardcover book. Be decisive. We're not handing out any awards for slick moves here, just get it done confidently. You've got this.

Let those pancakes cook until you can see that there's no more wet batter in there. It might take you a few tries on this griddle to get a feel for the timing, the heat and the texture you want. Every pancake is different and it's just a matter of what you like.

The same thing goes for the size. I should have mentioned that when you were pouring the batter back in Step 6, but you can think about it when you pour the next batch. There are no wrong answers. If you prefer a hotcake to a short stack or plate-covering flapjack to a silver dollar, it's all up to you and/or that girl who stayed over last night who is ruining that really nice coffee you just brewed from freshly ground beans by putting a half gallon of milk and a bunch of sugar in it. It's Allison, right? No, I think it's Amanda. Anna? Right. It's probably Anna. Most people are named Anna. Shit, maybe it's Hannah. No, it's probably Anna.

8 When both sides are cooked real good, start stacking up those pancakes on a warm plate. You can cover the stack with a fresh paper towel to trap that heat and moisture in.

This is the point in your pancake journey where you become a machine. You'll want to start cranking out those cakes quickly so you can eat 'em while they're hot. A courteous host will even serve the first round to their guest, lover or partner while more cakes are cooking.

In my experience, the second round to come off the griddle is a better stack; they're cooked better, they've got a better shape, and they're probably a better example of your craftsmanship. If you want Annie to think more highly of your skill level and to have a better experience at the breakfast table,[127] then you can stack and cover the first round on that side plate to save it for yourself, then serve her some refined, fluffy, killer cakes from the second or third round.

On the other hand, if you're still thinking about what she did to that coffee, chances are she won't appreciate the difference between the first and second stacks. Just get those pancakes over there so she has a knife and fork in her hands so she can

---

[127] I presume you already set the table properly for breakfast according to the place settings guide found earlier in the book. You will need a larger plate than the one shown in that presentation, but I didn't have a clean one when I took those photos.

focus on eating instead of monitoring her socials and curating her personal brand.

9 I am very much a purist when it comes to presentation. I want my pancakes to look like a cartoon picture of pancakes when they're on that plate: three pancakes high with a square slice of butter atop each one and covered in warm maple syrup that has been poured in a small circle over the center of that top butter slice[128] so it flows out in multiple directions and begins to pool around the pancakes. *Mmmm hmmm, I ga-ron-tee!*[129]

As I eat them, I'll cut 'em up and eventually move that butter all over 'em as it melts. But again, that's up to you.

You can also go down the road of adding other stuff like fresh berries, a dusting of powdered

---

[128] To be clear, there is a butter slice on top of each pancake, so two of them are sandwiched between the warm pancakes and they melt as you eat your way to them.

[129] Cajun accent

sugar, whipped cream, some kind of preserves, hazelnut spread,[130] or whatever. But I don't cotton to that style of hotel breakfast nonsense. I ain't into all them fancy fixins. It's just not me.

I keep it simple and classic. I'm not at all opposed to some scrambled eggs on the side with a small glass of freshly squeezed orange juice, and add some bacon[131] if that's your style.

Some mornings you might need a spicy Bloody Mary to complete the spread. If you had an awesome night and pitched a good drunk, you might as well keep the party going. You can really make a meal out of that kick in the pants.

Finally, a step that goes without saying: Sit down at the table with Annie, look her in the eyes when you impress her with your knowledge of the presidents, and be sure to take the time to savor your delicious pancake breakfast.

You earned this.[132]

---

[130] Nutella

[131] The Candy of the Barnyard™

[132] Don't forget to like and subscribe.

Online supplement

A clickable collection of this book's footnote links
and additional reference materials can be found at
www.kcomposite.com/howtoget

Index

Notes

Souvenir Stickers

Autographs